Mrs and the Blowing Day

Helen Morgan

Illustrated by Shirley Hughes

SIMON & SCHUSTER

LONDON • SYDNEY • NEW YORK • TOKYO • SINGAPORE • TORONTO

First published in Great Britain in 1968 by Faber and Faber Limited
This edition published in Great Britain in 1991 by Simon & Schuster
Young Books.

Set in 13pt Meridien by Goodfellow & Egan, Cambridge
Printed and bound in Great Britain by
The Guernsey Press Co. Ltd, Guernsey, Channel Islands

Simon & Schuster Young Books
Simon & Schuster Ltd
Wolsey House
Wolsey Road
Hemel Hempstead HP2 4SS

BRITISH LIBRARY CATALOGUING IN PUBLICATION DATA
available

ISBN 0 7500 0401 0
ISBN 0 7500 0402 9 Pbk

Contents

1 Mrs Pinny starts the washing   5

2 The wind makes a little more mischief   13

3 Mr Pinny is late for work   19

4 A bit of bother in Bunbridge   25

5 A sheet in the wind   31

6 Mrs Pinny sets out to deliver the washing   38

7 A pram in the sky   44

8 Mr Miskin is cross again   51

9 The windy wild day blows away   56

1

Mrs Pinny starts the washing

It was a beautiful bright and blowing day – a windy, wonderful washing day. The clouds were splashes of frothy suds and the sun was a piece of yellow soap in the blue deep bowl of the sky.

Little Mrs Pinny, the weekly washerwoman, flung open her bedroom lattice and sang when she saw the morning. Mr Pinny, snoozing still and bundled up in the blankets, heard her song through his snory sleep and almost woke up for a moment. He knew what the singing meant. His wife would go washing and splashing and sploshing and rinsing and wringing and pegging and singing from sooner than breakfast till later than long after tea.

Down the winding, steep-stepped stairs went Mrs Pinny, in her floppy old felt slippers. In the cosy kitchen she woke up the fire with a poke in the ribs and set the kettle to boil.

Then she slippered out to the scullery and started to fill the copper. Buckets and buckets of water she took, from the one tall, brass-bright tap, sploshing and sloshing it into the copper's cauldron. When the copper was full, Mrs Pinny knelt on the cold stone floor to light the fire.

Soon the screwed paper was leaping with light and the snap-crackling twigs were ablaze. In went the coal, the fire door was shut and the copper was left to itself.

By now, in the kitchen, the kettle was singing on the big, black-leaded stove. Mrs Pinny washed her hands and put the old brown teapot to warm.

One cup of tea she drank, all by herself, in secret, sniffing it, sipping it sugary slowly. Then she poured Mr Pinny a cup and buttered him two arrowroot biscuits.

"Unk," he said, when she put the tray down by the bed and the grunt was meant to be "Thank you".

By the time Mrs Pinny had shaken the rag rug and banged the big doormat, emptied the ashes, brushed over the grate, rubbed up the fire-irons and swept and dusted the kitchen, the copper was steaming well.

"I'm starting," she shouted up the stairs and Mr Pinny knew it meant "Get your own breakfast". He didn't want any breakfast yet, so he buried his head again. Mr Pinny was Ed the engine-driver when he went out to work, and this day, this wonderful washing day, he was not on duty until the afternoon. So he hid his head to shut out the sound of his wife at work in the steamy, sud-smelling scullery.

Three tubs Mrs Pinny set against the whitewashed wall, close to the great iron mangle – one for the blue-bag, one for the starch and one for the clear, cold rinsing.

Then she started to sort out the washing. Shirts here, socks there, pinafores, petticoats, pyjamas and pillow-slips – all had their proper places. Here were the towels in a tumbled heap and the sheets flowing over the floor. Here were the handkerchiefs, there were the tablecloths, and the woollens were put in a basket.

Soon the floor was strewn with the weekly wash from half a dozen houses. Mrs Pinny knew every cloth and clout of it, from the big old sheet with the patch in the middle that belonged to the Smiths in Sheep Street to Lucy Larkin's little sock with the tiny hole in the toe. She never mistook a Mills for a Martin nor folded a Fraser into a Biggins bundle.

When the washing was sorted, down to the last baby's bib, Mrs Pinny lifted the round wooden lid that covered the boiling copper.

Steam swooshed out and swept over her. She was lost in a warm, moist mist. She dipped a hand-bowl into the bubbling water and began to fill the tin bath that stood on the table close by.

Scalding hot from the copper and spiteful cold from the tap, the water went into the bath. Then the shirts went in and the rubbing board and the soap and Mrs Pinny's hands.

Rubbing and scrubbing, the washerwoman stood there and sang. Her rosy face grew rosier still and her arms were as boiled as beetroots. There was boiling and blueing and starching and rinsing and wringing the whole morning long.

Up in the day-bright bedroom, Ed-the-engine-driver Pinny stirred and mumbled in his sleep. He was hungry now, but not hungry enough to get up and make his own breakfast.

He opened one eye and looked at the chattering clock.

"She must be well on with the wash by now," he thought, when he saw the time. "If I lie here long enough and keep quiet, she'll bring me my breakfast in bed."

It was twenty to nine, it was warm, it was fine and the children were going to school. Five of them, racing, shouting and chasing, came down Lambkins Lane to catch the little green country bus at Cobblers Corner. They were Eileen and Ronnie and Josie and Johnny and last, but not least, Henrietta.

Mrs Pinny was in her garden when the children ran past her cottage. She was reaching up to the line to see if the first load of washing was dry.

The wind had died down to a whisper and the looping clothes-line drooped with the weight of the wash.

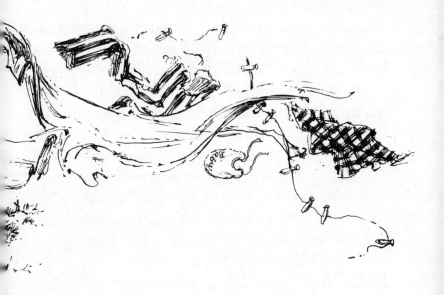

Tiptoe tall, Mrs Pinny reached up to a striped pyjama sleeve. The waiting wind leapt up and snatched it away. Mrs Pinny clutched at the prop. It shifted and slipped and the wicked wind whipped the clothes-line up and away.

Like festival streamers, the washing went streaking towards the sparkling autumn sky. Shirts leapt about, loose pegs all came out and a small flock of socks flew happily over the hedge.

"Hey!" cried a child. "Hey, look! It's raining washing."

Five giggling children stopped in the lane and collected the scattered socks. The wind held its breath and watched them and the clothes-line

11

came drifting down from the dizzying tree-tops.

Teasing and chaffing, the children came laughing in at Mrs Pinny's gate. They sorted the socks into pairs and helped her pick up the pegs.

The wind wandered off down the slope of the leaning field and came hurrying back again with the sound of the slow school bell.

"You'll be late! You'll be late!" cried Mrs Pinny. "Take some sweeties with you."

She bustled into the cottage to fetch the toffee tin. Small hands reached out and were filled and the children raced out to the lane. They knew they had missed the bus and would have to go by the field path. The sound of their cheerful, chewy good-byes came drifting back to Mrs Pinny as they went, with the wind, down the long green slope to the village.

They squeezed through the kissing-gate at Cobblers Cross, ran down the lane in a straggling, hand-holding line and galloped into the playground. They should have had a black mark for being late, but they said they had stopped to help an old lady so they all had a star instead.

The wind, that had gone to school with them, laughed to itself and went off to look for more mischief.

2

The wind makes a little more mischief

In the town of Bunbridge, a mile away, the shops were waking up. Doors were unlocked, shelves were restocked and counters were dusted and polished. Blank blinds were lifted, shutters were shifted and stalls were set out in the sun.

The wandering wind was trapped in the alleys and baffled by high brick walls. It rattled the lids of the clattering bins and shook all the ill-fitting gates. It howled round the houses, blew under the doors, moaned at the windows and sneaked up through the floors.

The little bus from Cobblers Green rumbled along the High Street and stopped in the Market Square. Mothers and aunties and grannies got off, clutching their shopping baskets. The wind went to meet them, twisting their skirts, tugging their scarf-ends, making them hold their hats.

Coming and going and to-ing and fro-ing, shoppers and stall-holders moved in a crowding, cheerful confusion. P.C. Samuel Spindleberry, lean as a bean-pole, stood in a doorway, keeping an eye on things.

Above the sound of the buying and selling, the good-humoured banter and shouting and yelling, could be heard the constant flap and slap of canvas. The restless wind was amusing itself with the hoods and skirts of the stalls.

Then, like a lion let loose, it roared across the Market, sending a scatter of dead leaves and litter dustily over the crowd. A tower of cardboard boxes collapsed in a heap and a pyramid of tinned beans toppled and fell, bruising the shins and clobbering the corns of the legs and feet close by.

Mr Miskin, the Stationmaster, on his way to Bunbridge Station, had his peaked and braided cap ripped rudely from his head. Sliding and skidding and saucepan-lidding, the splendid, gilded cap ran away down the road.

Plump as a dumpling, Mr Miskin ran after it. It was kicked, it was tossed, it was caught, it was lost by the helpful, hurrying crowd. Dusty and dented it landed, at last, by the patient, polished boots of P.C. Spindleberry.

The policeman picked it up and looked at it.

"Somebody's lost his hat," he said.

"Somebody's going to be sorry."

The Stationmaster puffed hurriedly, hatless, towards him.

"Thank you, Constable," he said. "I thought I should never catch it,"

"It's a bit dusty, Mr Miskin, sir," said P.C. Spindleberry, trying to clean the cap on his coat-sleeve.

"It's only my working cap," said Mr Miskin. "I've another for special occasions."

Holding the cap down hard on his head

lest the wind should want it again, the Stationmaster hurried out of the Square. Along the High Street he went and up the steep, stony slope of the station yard to his tiny, tidy office.

Before he went in he paused by the open door to look back at the town of Bunbridge. It lay sprawled in the autumn sunlight, a crazy maze of cobbled streets and a muddling huddle of houses.

"Nice little town," said Mr Miskin warmly. "Nice, quiet, friendly little place. Nice day, too." He took off his battered cap and looked at it. "We could do without this wind, though," he added.

For answer, the wind slammed the office door shut in his face.

Snoozily snug in the blankets, Mr Pinny turned on his back and thought about not getting up. He was no longer hollow with hunger because Mrs Pinny had taken him up a big brimming cup of freshly brewed tea and a bulging bacon sandwich.

"She's a good old thing," he thought, biting into the bacon. "She knows I like having breakfast in bed." It never once entered his silly old head that she wanted him out of the way.

Comfortably full, he had cosied down in the covers again and dozed the morning away. Now

16

he was also awake once more and feeling pleasantly peckish.

"Perhaps I'll get up," he thought, "and see what she's doing about dinner."

Mrs Pinny wasn't doing anything about dinner. She was walking along the garden path with the third load of washing lying meekly in the basket.

The wind was crouching quiet in a corner, among the orange flames of the last, late, straggling nasturtiums. It let out its breath with a little sigh and a strand of hair tickled the tip of Mrs Pinny's nose.

She lowered the line and picked up a pillow-slip. One peg, two pegs and it was on the line. At once the wind leapt into it, blowing it out like a big balloon.

Mrs Pinny took up a shirt and hung it up by its tail. It came quickly alive and started to writhe. With a twist and a twirl, a flick and a curl, it lifted its sleeves and looped itself over the line.

Mrs Pinny clicked her tongue and disentangled the shirt. The wind stood still and waited.

In a little while half the line was hung with shirts and pillow-slips, towels and table-cloths, all shifting and wriggling a little – but not too much.

Mrs Pinny picked up the basket and carried it a little way down the path. The wind caught the corner of Mrs Pinny's warm and woolly shawl and flapped it over her head. Down went the basket, tipping and tumbling – and down went Mrs Pinny. The sun was shut out and the sky was shut out and her mouth was full of wool.

She struggled up and pulled the shawl from her face. She was cross, she was crumpled, her hair was all rumpled and some of the washing was dirty. A towel and a sheet bore the marks of her feet. She had stepped on them when she fell.

She carried them back to the scullery and washed them clean again.

The wind was waiting for her. As Mrs Pinny lifted the sheet to peg it on the line the wind gave a long, low whistle and sprang towards her. It caught hold of the wide, wet sheet and folded it, close and uncomfortable, right round Mrs Pinny.

She was cramped, she was damped, she was draggled. She was trapped, she was wrapped as she struggled. She was a weird, white, groaning ghost in the warm, October garden.

3

Mr Pinny is late for work

Up in the bedroom the loose lattice clattered because it was battered each time the wind went by. Mr Pinny had changed his mind about getting up. He was trying to dig himself deep down into sleep again, but the lattice creaking and shifting and squeaking drove his dreams away.

Grumbling, he fumbled his way out of the blankets and went to close the window.

The diamond panes glinted, the sleepy man squinted and looked down into the garden.

A sheet shaped like a someone was struggling along the path. It had half a face, a tumble of hair, one waving hand and two black, stumbling feet.

In a terrible fright, Mr Pinny hid his head in his hands.

Then the sheet started shouting and the shout sounded like his wife. He peeped between his fingers and saw Mrs Pinny's face, red as a raspberry, glaring up at him.

"Come down, you great silly," she shouted. "Come down at once and help me out of this before the rheumatics get me."

Just for a moment Mr Pinny felt daft. He stared at the ghost that wasn't a ghost – then he laughed . . . and he laughed . . . and he laughed. He laughed till his middle hurt and the tears squeezed themselves out of his eyes. He laughed till all his breath was lost and he had none left for anything heartier than a gurgle.

Gasping, he put on his shoes and his overcoat and went weakly down the stairs.

Mrs Pinny had hobbled to the scullery door, still tightly trapped in the sheet. Mr Pinny hastily put his face straight and went outside to unwind her.

"Don't drag the sheet in the dirt!" she snapped.

Mr Pinny found a crumpled corner and pulled the sheet wetly towards him. He held his mouth shut, tight as a lid on a biscuit tin, so the laughter wouldn't escape and make his wife crosser. He was a larky sort of man and he often laughed when he shouldn't.

As Mr Pinny gathered the soggy stuff in his hands, Mrs Pinny turned round and round and the sheet was slowly, slowly unwound. Mr

Pinny bundled it up and went out to put it back in the wicker basket.

When he went back to the kitchen he found Mrs Pinny fiercely poking the fire. The kettle spat like a cat as she jerked it on to the hob. Then it settled down and began its sibilant singing.

Under the swift jab and stab of Mrs Pinny's poker, the fire, that was slow, began to glow and sizzle and grow too hot for her to stand near.

Blinking a little, she knelt in the heat on the

hearthrug.

Wonderful warmth wafted over her and the damp steamed out of her clothes and the chill crept out of her bones. She turned herself round and toasted the other side. In a little while she was quite her old cheerful self again.

"What's for dinner?" asked Mr Pinny, seeing her smile come back.

"Cold beef and bubble and squeak," she said. "And tea and batter pudding with strawberry jam. Get yourself dressed. I'll fetch the frying-pan."

Out in the garden the wind found its sport was spoiled. It went sulkily over the rooftop and blew the smoke back down the chimney.

It was a golden afternoon. The light leaned sideways on the distant hills and the sky was a clear, clean blue.

Ed-the-engine-driver Pinny had had his dinner and his three cups of tea, put on his uniform and polished his boots. Now he was cycling the gently sloping mile down Lambkins Lane to Bunbridge Station.

The whirr of his speeding wheels, the tingling touch of the wind on his face, the sparkle of sunlight on the lake below, made Mr Pinny want to sing.

He opened his mouth and let out a shout of

music. The sound of his song blew away behind him and was lost in the long and empty lane.

Mr Pinny swooped round a bend in the road, ringing his bell with wild delight. The wind swung round and came bustling up behind him.

Faster and faster the wheels went round, as the bicycle sped downhill. Spinning along and singing his song, Mr Pinny almost believed he was flying. The wind seemed to curve itself about his shoulders, gently cushioning, pushing him on, giving him a strange sensation of strength.

He took his hands off the handlebars like a larky boy showing off in front of his friends.

It was then that the wind *really* pushed him. Not straight, not smooth, but sideways it sent him, skidding giddily all askew. Mr Pinny clutched at the turning handlebars and tried to straighten the swerving wheel. It was no use. The wind and the wheel had their own wicked way and the bicycle leapt, like a startled pony, over the shallow ditch and hurled itself into the hedge.

Cuffed and buffeted, snatched and scratched, Mr Pinny sat in a muddle of metal while the back wheel whizzed and whirred without travelling half a yard.

The wind was no more than a sigh in the spinney now. Torn and tawny, the crisp leaves lay, waiting for wandering feet to come and crackle through them. The golden day dawdled on and no one came down the lane.

Dazed and mazy, Mr Pinny pulled himself up at last. He felt himself carefully, to find out if he was broken. He wasn't. He wasn't even cracked or chipped.

He picked up his wayward bicycle and examined it all over. It seemed to be quite all right.

Cautiously he climbed on to it and rode, with great care, down the hill to Bunbridge Station.

4

A bit of bother in Bunbridge

"WHERE IS PINNY?" roared Mr Miskin, coming out of his office for the umpteenth time and looking along the platform.

Nobody knew where Ed-the-engine-driver Pinny was and nobody thought of trying to find out.

The Stationmaster pulled out his large, reliable watch and looked at it. Then he looked at the engine which was simmering quietly in the siding.

"Another two minutes," thundered Mr Miskin, "and the Market will be closed. Five minutes after that the passengers will start arriving. They'll want their train! They'll *expect* their train! They're *entitled* to their train! WHERE IS PINNY?"

The engine hissed and a warm white mist drifted across the platform.

The Town Hall clock began, without warning, to tell the town the time. "Three," it said in its big, bold, booming voice. One after the other, from tall church towers, four clocks said it was wrong. Chime after chime disputed the time and the minutes ticked away.

The Market was closing now. Not a watch, not a ring, not a ball of string, not a peach, not a pie, not a single thing must be sold after three o'clock.

It was P.C. Spindleberry's duty, today, to see that nothing was.

He walked, with his hands behind him, along the cluttered, littered pavement. The stall-holders turned their backs on him, regretfully packing up. Here and there a crafty customer hung about, hoping to make a law-breaking bargain for what was left on the stalls.

Shopkeepers stood in their doorways, warming themselves in the sunlight, smiling and rubbing their hands. Now that the Market was closed, their customers would come back to them.

Old men with big, brisk brooms came whistling and bustling into the Market Square. They swooshed and pushed the rubbish into small, untidy piles along the edge of the kerb. The wind, that had been somewhere else for the past half-hour, rushed gustily round the corner and swooped on a heap of sweepings.

Papers and packets and labels and tickets and just plain, ordinary dirt, flew, like a flock of frightened sparrows, all over the emptying Square.

Coughing and snishing and wheezing and swishing, the sweepers started again and the wind went quietly away and left them to it.

Bunbridge Station was busy. Hand-bagging, gloving, shuffling and shoving, the Market Day crowd pushed itself through the narrow doorway of the entrance hall and on to the draughty platform. Mr Miskin, in a ticket-collector's cap, punched little holes in squares of green cardboard and muttered under his breath. The ticket-collector was being a porter and the porter had gone to look for Mr Pinny. The 3.25, Bunbridge to Tumbleton, was definitely going to run late.

"Where's the train?" said the passengers, surprised not to see it where it usually was.

It was still in the sidings, of course, waiting for its driver.

"COME TO SPAIN," said a bold, black message on a picture crazy with colour. All the passengers stared at it, but none of them bothered to go.

They were murmuring and mumbling and

very nearly grumbling when Mr Pinny rode into the station yard. Behind him came the porter, on a borrowed bicycle. The ticket-collector rolled down his shirt sleeves and put on his coat again. Mr Miskin changed his cap and bellowed, "Come into my office!"

"I'm sorry I'm late," gasped Mr Pinny. "The wind blew me off my bike." His hat was askew and his hair was all rumpled. He was dusty and thirsty and dreadfully crumpled. The Stationmaster almost felt sorry for him, he looked so blown about. Then, out of the corner of his eye, he caught sight of the staring clock on the stale-cream-coloured wall. It was 3.23 and the train was due out in two minutes.

"You should have been on duty half an hour ago," he said, in his most official voice. "Go on, man, get a move on. You've got a train to catch."

She was getting up steam, the Market Day Special, puffing herself up with power and pride, making ready to take her regulars home.

The thoughtful porter brought Mr Pinny a cup of waiting-room tea and told him not to worry.

"Worse things happen at sea," he said, which didn't make much sense except to the Stationmaster, who suddenly had an idea.

"HERE IS AN ANNOUNCEMENT! HERE IS

AN ANNOUNCEMENT!" cried a terrible, twisted voice. The Stationmaster was playing at being a ship's captain. He was up on the bridge between the port and starboard platforms, bellowing through a loud hailer.

"The train now arriving at Platform One is the 3.30 Special to Tumbleton, calling at Cobblers Halt, Sage Green, Rumden, Plumden and Slate.

The train now arriving at Platform One is the THREE-THIRTY to Tumbleton."

There was a babbling and gabbling among the passengers. Their faces showed surprise and relief and here and there annoyance.

"They've changed the time of the train," they said. "They might have let us know."

"We needn't have rushed to catch it," they said, "we might have had time for a cuppa."

Ed-the-engine-driver Pinny brought the train out of the siding and on to the Tumbleton track. She came past the slope at the end of the platform, blowing out dragon's breath. Slowly the glassy-eyed carriages slipped past the waiting crowd. Then the engine sighed and stopped moving, and the carriages came to a juddering, shuddering halt.

Poking and jabbing and corner-seat grabbing, the Market Day crowd climbed aboard. Spiteful baskets and bulky baggage, peculiar parcels and lumpy luggage, they settled into their seats.

Then, with a wild, weird shriek of delight, the little train was away. The wind went down and roared past her windows, sending her smoke trail steaming across the afternoon sky.

5

A sheet in the wind

Mrs Pinny was pleased with herself. In spite of the naughty wind, she had most of her washing dry. There was just one sheet, one single sheet, to peg on the empty line. She took it out while the wind was quiet and pinned it with plenty of pegs.

Then she went back to her cottage and looked at the work she had done.

The mangle was wiped down and hidden now, under an old Turkish towel. Neat as a bundle of newly-delivered newspapers, the mangled clothes stood in three high piles on the well-scrubbed scullery table.

Before he went off on his bicycle, Mr Pinny had helped her pull the sheets. Corner to corner and corner again, he pulled and she pulled, till the sheets were stretched and straight. Then meet in the middle, he hold and she fold and meet in the middle again. Now they had been through the mangle and were waiting to have their tops ironed.

In the kitchen the table was spread with the thick old ironing blanket and over it the scorch-marked ironing cloth. Two big flat-irons were upended on the hob, warming their satin-smooth faces in front of the fire. The iron-holder hung by a loop of blue wool from a hook near the toasting-fork.

The washing-day wind came blowing up from Bunbridge and snatched at the sheet in Mrs Pinny's garden. It whipped it and ripped it and wrenched half its pegs away. Then it left the long garden, with a litter of leaves on the lawn, whisking itself away to the woods to torment the leaning trees.

This was the moment Mr Miskin had chosen to play at being a sea captain. He was up on the bridge, making a speech to his passengers.

In Mrs Pinny's garden the sheet was a wet sail slapping and the prop was a broken mast but the sea captain knew nothing about that . . . and Mrs Pinny knew nothing about the 3.25 that had just become the 3.30.

She was in the kitchen, singing away to herself and doing the ironing. What was too damp she dried on a piece of string slung under the mantelshelf. What was too dry she damped with a sprinkle of water and rolled it up for a while.

She tested the irons with the tip of her wetted finger and listened to the sizzle the moisture made. Hot for the handkerchiefs, cool for the silks, barely warm for the woollens, the smooth-faced irons slid to and fro over the weekly wash. The collars came up as stiff as cardboard and the starchy pillow-slips were shining smooth. The coloured clothes were clean and bright and the sheets and tablecloths snowy white. Backwards and forwards the swift iron went, pleating and pressing, sleeking, caressing the washed and waiting garments. Tuck, frill and pocket, hemline and plaquet, all came under its warm and wonderful spell. Rumple and crumple were

skilfully eased, wrinkles released and creases uncreased and each carefully folded piece was gently placed on the clothes-horse, to finish in front of the fire.

Then Mrs Pinny heard the hurrying train. With a chuffity-chuff and a huffity-puff it rushed through the field on the other side of the lane. She heard it scream as it entered the hole in the hill. It roared through the tunnel and rattled away to Sage Green.

"What's wrong with my clock, then?" said Mrs Pinny, taking and shaking the tick-tocking thing. "It's nigh on five minutes fast."

It wasn't, of course. The train was five minutes late. Poor Mrs Pinny! When she leaves her house at half after four she will be too late to catch the train to Bunbridge.

Now the wind had a nip in it and the day was beginning to fade. The sun had slipped down and the deep, deep blue was almost rinsed out of the sky.

Mrs Pinny brought the kettle out from the back of the stove and pushed it over the hob. She put the brown teapot to warm and set herself a tray on the empty side of the table. She changed the cold iron for a hot one and went on with her washday work. The iron-holder slipped and scorched itself on the roast-hot iron. Mrs Pinny's hand slipped with it and her knuckles were slightly singed, but she was so used to the heat she hardly noticed it. She swooped on the sheet spread on the table and speedily smoothed it out. Six sheets she did, then she stopped and had her tea.

All the while, in the garden, the last sheet clung to the prop, one peg only holding it on to the line.

In Cobblers Green the church clock's chime said, "Stop lessons now. It's going-home time."

Girls and boys started making a noise the moment the school bell rang. They crammed their satchels with this and that, slammed shut their desks, snatched a glove or a hat, dragged on their coats, crumpling their suits and went home in somebody else's boots.

The ones who lived in the village had no need to hurry. They could race and shout and hang about long after the others had gone, in the little green bus.

Five children climbed down when the bus stopped at Cobblers Corner. They waited and waved till the bus disappeared and then ran off towards their cottage homes. They were Eileen and Ronnie and Josie and Johnny and last, but not least, Henrietta.

"Mrs Pinny's washing's blown off again," said Josie, when she saw the sheet draped droopily round the prop.

"Shall we go and tell her?" suggested Henrietta. "She might give us some more sweets."

"Greedy pig," said Ronnie. "You had enough this morning,"

"Let's go and get it off the line for her," suggested Eileen, going in through the garden gate.

They lowered the prop and the sheet fell, flop, in a heap on the crazy path. Now they could reach the peg. One of them pulled it out and they looped the sheet baggily over the sagging line. Then they pushed the prop up a little to clear the sheet from the ground.

It was then that the wind came, wild as a bull newly broken out of its pen. It crashed through the thin thorn hedge and went billowing, bellowing, into the loose-hung sheet. The sheet shifted and lifted, leapt lightly up from the line and went to play with the wind in the meadow down the hill.

The children cried out and quickly covered their mouths with their hands to keep themselves quiet. With one accord they turned and ran out of the garden, leaving the gate to swing itself shut behind them.

6

Mrs Pinny sets out to deliver the washing

Mrs Pinny had had her tea and finished off the ironing. The irons were cooling now, on the slabstone back of the copper, and the kitchen table was wearing, once more, its fringed and crimson cloth.

Swiftly, deftly, the old woman folded the ironed and fire-warmed washing. Three separate piles she made of it, on the plushy crimson cover. Each pile was wrapped in a piece of sheet and wound about with string. A scribbled name on a scrap of paper was pinned to each cumbersome bundle. There was one for the Smiths of Sheep Street, one for the Larkins of Marrow Lane and one for the Biggins of Broadway.

When the bundles were ready, Mrs Pinny collapsed the clothes-horse, turned down the damper on the chimney and shut the little fire door in front of the stove. Then she pulled back the fender, turned back the hearthrug and made sure the kettle was full.

The clock on the mantelshelf said twenty-five minutes past four but Mrs Pinny thought it was five minutes fast. So she took her time over tidying her hair and fixing her bonnet. It was her second-best bonnet and not a very good fit. It looked like a black straw coal-scuttle, hung about with black crêpe ribbons.

The crown was padded with paper but the bonnet was still rather loose. So the

washerwoman took a long, thin, silver-knobbed hatpin from the pin-cushion hung on the wall. With a jab and a stab she drove it clean through bonnet and topknot and then she put on her coat. It was black as her hat and had a short, beaded cape to keep her old shoulders warm.

When she was ready, she went out to the shed to fetch her washerwoman's pram. It, too, was black – shiny and black as a funeral coach and pretty much the same shape. It had come from a very grand house and the dribbling, bubbling, thumb-sucking baby that used to sit in it was now a very grand gentleman, who lived in a castle and wore a coronet. Mrs Pinny wondered, sometimes, what his capped and starchy Nanny would have said, had she known that the pram that once carried an Earl now carried the weekly washing.

When the laundry for Smith and Larkins and Biggins was safely lodged in the pram, Mrs Pinny locked the scullery door and set off for Cobblers Halt.

Twelve miles away, in Tumbleton Station, the Market Special was safely in the sidings. Ed-the-engine-driver Pinny had had a mug of tea and a stale cheese roll in the dark green gloom of the waiting-room and was half-way back to Bunbridge. He was tunnelling under Cobblers Hill in the flashing, deafening dark, preparing to slow down and slide into Cobblers Halt at four thirty-six preciscly.

At four thirty-six Mrs Pinny should have been standing on the narrow wooden platform with the big, high-wheeled pram. She and the pram always travelled in the guard's van the downhill mile to Bunbridge. This day, though, this darking, wind-larking day, Mrs Pinny wasn't waiting at Cobblers Halt.

Five minutes late she came out of her gate and pushed the pram down Lambkins Lane. Unhurried, unworried, she thought she had plenty of time. It was only three minutes' walk, by the field path, to the railway line and the Halt.

Rattling and clattering, the hard-rimmed wheels rumbled over the rough little lane. The pram hood was up because it was stuck and couldn't be put down. Larkins lay under the hood with Biggins beneath it and Smith of Sheep Street sat at the handle end. Mrs Pinny shifted her bulging brown leather hold-all and tried to push Smith a little more under the hood. The light was leaving the day too fast and the air had the feel of rain.

A few yards from her garden gate Mrs Pinny swung the pram off the lane and into the wired-in, well-worn station footpath. It was then that she heard the train.

Clumsily, bumpily, Mrs Pinny began to run down the path. It was not very wide, there was wire on each side and no room to make a mistake. One little swerve, the tiniest curve — and the pram would hit the fence.

She was half-way to Cobblers Halt when she saw the white spread of sheet, hung like a hood on a gorse bush. She knew it at once for her own because of the pear-shaped patch at one end where Mr Pinny's fidgety foot had poked a pear-shaped hole

Mrs Pinny stopped running and pushing and rushing the washing along the narrow path. She

stood quite still and tried to catch her breath. She couldn't think how she had come to forget the sheet was out in the garden. She couldn't think how it had come unpegged and carried itself off to the meadow, but she was far too thrifty to leave it there on the gorse bush. The four thirty-six would have to go without her today. She must rescue her sheet and catch the five fifty-five.

She went slowly back the way she had come, dragging the wobbling pram behind her. She hadn't room enough to turn round, so she travelled over the bumpy ground like a horse with an unwilling cart.

Ed-the-engine-driver Pinny stopped the train at the Halt.

"Where's my missis, then?" he said as he slid past the empty platform. Then, away across the field, he saw the pram.

Fred, the fireman, saw it, too, nearly three minutes away.

"She's not coming, she's going," he said. "Get a move on, now. We can't wait. You can't run *all* your trains five minutes late."

7

A pram in the sky

Mrs Pinny dragged the pramful of washing out of the public footpath and into Lambkins Lane. Five children, playing a game without a name where Lambkins Lane was lost and became no more than a track through the woods, saw her and stopped pretending. They were Eileen and Ronnie and Josie and Johnny and last, but not least, Henrietta.

"She's seen the sheet," they said and stood closer together.

"She won't know it was us," said Eileen. "She'll think it was the wind."

"It *was* the wind," said the others, but Eileen still felt guilty.

"Let's go and help her get it off the gorse bush," she suggested and started to run down the lane.

With a jump and a shout the rest turned about and hopped happily after her.

Mrs Pinny, hearing, saw them and waved her hand in greeting.

Confused and perplexed and wondering what next, Mr Pinny at Cobblers Halt watched his wife going backwards. Then he saw her wave her hand and took it to mean she was going home again. In another moment the four thirty-six would have been the four thirty-seven. With a steamy sigh and a sad little cry, the train drew away from the platform.

The wind had grown tired of teasing the trees in the wood. It came running low down the lane, whipping the children like tops and sending them spinning. They held on to their hats and their heads and their ears, but the tears in their eyes were not really tears. Laughing and rosy, they cuddled up cosy, under the chestnut tree.

Mrs Pinny was parking the pram by the gate that led to the field. She felt the wind smite her mightily in the middle of her back, almost knocking her off her feet and into the big old pram.

Gasping, and grasping the pram, she stood, while the wind went wild and leapt under the hood. The five children under the chestnut tree cried out at what happened next. If they hadn't seen it, they would not have believed it – but the wind took the pram full of washing and

heaved it, all anyhow, into the air. Hedge-high, tree-high, up into the sky, went the big, black pram, with the wild-eyed washerwoman hanging on to the handle.

Shrieking and screaming, the children went streaming along the lane, like scattered pieces of paper. Scarves flying, hats lost, the five of them crossed the lane and ran into the field.

High overhead, Mrs Pinny flew like a witch without a broomstick, pushing her witch's washing in her witch's wonderful pram. A blackbird saw her and winged away, whistling in wild alarm. Mrs Pinny looked down and saw the trembling top of a tree. In a terrible fright, she shut her eyes, tight – and told herself she was dreaming.

Stumbling and falling the children ran, calling her from the field. The wind took their voices and twisted them and made them into a moan. "Mrs Pinny!" they called. "Come back! Come back! . . . Come back, Mrs Pinny, come back."

They were snagged, they were snatched, they were jabbed, stabbed and scratched as they scrambled their way through the brambles, but they went from one field to another still watching the washerwoman. Through bush and through briar, even over barbed wire, they followed the way the wind blew her.

She was well away from the lane by now and over the railway embankment. Below her, the smoking snake of the four thirty-six chugged cheerfully down to Bunbridge.

A soldier, a nurse and a little fat man happened to glance out of the windows as the pram flew by in the sky.

The fat little man fell right off his seat, the soldier snorted and shut his eyes and the nurse made a noise like a nightmare.

Then the soldier put his head out of the window and shouted and the nurse put her

48

head out of the window and screamed and the fat little man just sat on the floor and held his head in his hands.

Windows went clattering down on their straps, passengers woke from their nice little naps, some cheered and some jeered and some waved their caps and some of them yelled for help.

Then one of them PULLED THE COMMUNICATION CORD!

Such a thing had never happened before when Mr Pinny was driving. He was not just perplexed, he was quite clearly vexed as he brought the train to a stop. All along its little length, heads were poked out of the windows. There were laughing faces and frightened faces and faces still half asleep. One or two of them even looked annoyed. All the heads were turned in the same direction, all the eyes were fixed on something up in the air.

Without a word, the fireman, the guard and the engine-driver looked to see what it was.

Not an albatross, an eclipse of the moon, a flying saucer, or a big balloon, not shooting stars or men from Mars, did Mr Pinny see, but a little old lady, dressed all in black pushing a pram through the sky.

"It's my missis," he gasped and felt himself shaking. His legs were just socks full of jelly.

Mrs Pinny was holding the pram handle firmly with both her hands. She held herself upright, she was looking straight in front of her. Her feet went briskly to and fro as she walked on the weight of the wind. With her eyes wide open and her mouth shut tight, she told herself she was quite all right. She was just an ordinary washerwoman, pushing the washing down the hill in a perfectly ordinary pram.

The tops of the trees were below her knees, but she refused to believe they were there. The wind was holding her up like a mother's hand holding a baby in a bath, but Mrs Pinny ignored it. A long way off, there were rooftops and chimneys spilling smoke. Mrs Pinny would not look at them. She would not look at the low, green fields nor hear the calling children. She would not see the panting train, stopped half-way between two stations. Her gaze was fixed on a little cloud, drifting darkly along not very far ahead. She was sure she would soon wake up and find herself on the ground.

So she turned out her toes and followed her nose and wheeled her pram full of washing along in the air.

8

Mr Miskin is cross again

The children decided to give up the chase at last. Breathless and draggled, they turned round and straggled slowly back up the hill. They knew that their Mums would be waiting for them, cross because they were late.

"They'll never believe us," said Eileen to Ronnie, and Josie and Johnny agreed. Henrietta said nothing and nobody bothered to ask her what she was thinking.

When they came to the field by the footpath, the five children stopped and looked at the sheet on the gorse bush.

"Let's get it off for her," said Eileen.

"What if she doesn't come back?" said Henrietta, because *that* was what she was thinking.

"SHUT UP!" cried Eileen and Ronnie, and "Don't be daft," said Josie and Johnny, and they all ran to pull at the sheet.

The gorse bush was prickly and they found out quite quickly that the sheet wouldn't shift without tearing. Then a bit of a breeze that was left behind when the wind went rushing away, puffed itself under the sheet and began to blow.

"Catch it!" cried Eileen as the sheet began slowly to rise. They could hear it was tearing and would need some repairing, but they pulled it away from the bush. They folded it, somehow, between them and carried it off to Mrs Pinny's garden. The shed seemed the best place to leave it, so they put it inside and slammed the door shut, to make sure it couldn't get out.

Then, singing and dancing, the children went prancing away up the lane, to their teas.

"WHERE IS PINNY?" shouted Mr Miskin. "What's he done with the four-twelve from Tumbleton?"

The four-twelve from Tumbleton (which became the four thirty-six at Cobblers Halt) was still half a mile outside Bunbridge Station. Ed-the-engine-driver Pinny, the fireman, Fred, and the guard, who was Jack, were still standing, gaping, down the track, while a little old lady, dressed all in black, was pushing a pram through the sky. They came to life at last and remembered they had a train-load of passengers who wanted to go to Bunbridge.

By the time the engine began to move the washerwoman was well ahead, her beaded cape streaming out behind her and her baggy skirts blown big as a crinoline.

The train went hurtling down the hill but Mrs Pinny went faster still and the trees bent over backwards to let her pass.

The passengers still had their heads stuck out of the windows, in spite of the warnings they must all have seen and read. The soldier was blinking, the nurse had stopped thinking and the little fat man was still sitting on the floor.

Mr Pinny was talking to himself as he handled the hurrying engine.

"I must have been hurt after all," he said. "I must have had a crack on the head, when the wind blew me off my bike. I didn't wake up. I still haven't woken up. I expect I shall wake up presently and find myself sitting in the ditch."

"She's changing course!" cried the fireman, Fred. "She's heading for the town."

The wind had swung Mrs Pinny round like a weather-cock and was blowing her away from the station towards the Market Square.

Mr Pinny smiled with his mouth but his eyes were like blue glass marbles. He was dreaming again. He was driving a train while his wife, in her second-best bonnet, was flying about like a bird. It was quite an amusing dream.

"It must have been quite a crack I gave myself," he thought. "I wonder how long I've been asleep?"

The train was coming into the station now. The Station-master stood waiting for it, ready to pounce on Ed-the-engine-driver Pinny. "Who does Pinny think he is?" he muttered. "What's he playing at?" he spluttered. "What right had *he* to go changing the time of the train?'

Then he saw the heads sticking out of the carriage windows.

"What's the matter with that lot?" he shouted. "Have they all taken leave of their senses? Don't they know that travelling with the head stuck out of the window is asking to have it knocked off?"

The porter stopped pushing his broom up and down the same little patch of platform. "They're looking at something," he said and stretched his neck, trying to see what it was.

He couldn't. Left Luggage and Ladies Waiting Room stood squarely in the way. He let the broom lean on a weighing-machine and went out to the cobbled yard in front of the station.

Before him, grey in the fading light, lay the huddled muddle of Bunbridge. Over it, low, lay a leaden sky heavy with hurrying clouds – and below the clouds, a little above the rooftops, flew a strange kind of carriage and what seemed to be a person. They were too far away for the porter to see them clearly.

"Father Christmas!" he said, surprised. Then he shook his head sadly. "Poor old chap must be losing his grip. He's come a couple of months too early."

Then he heard the swift, impatient scuffle of footsteps behind him. The train was in. The passengers were coming. Like a buzz of bees from a hive, they brushed past the porter. Among them were a nurse and a soldier and a little fat man, grimed and grubby from sitting too long on the floor.

"There she is!" they cried, waving their arms and pointing, as they streamed down the hill to the town.

"What's up with them, then?" gasped the porter, knocked sideways by their passing.

Pink as a plateful of strawberry blancmange, Mr Miskin came bustling breathlessly out of the station.

"Pinny's gone off his head," he panted. "We shall have to find a replacement. He thinks he saw his wife on top of a tree, with a pram."

"Poor old Ed," said the porter, clicking his tongue. "What an imagination! It wasn't his wife he saw. It was Father Christmas. I've just seen him myself, flying over the Market Square."

9

The windy wild day blows away

P.C. Samuel Spindleberry, pounding his beat on his size thirteen feet, was thinking about buttered crumpets. All the gold had gone out of the day. Rain clouds bulged over Bunbridge like a tumble of old feather beds.

P.C. Spindleberry turned into Market Square and stopped in surprise. In the empty space of the market place a small, gaping crowd had gathered. They were all staring skywards with astonishment on their faces. The policeman looked up, between the moving pattern of the lime trees, and saw a little old woman, dressed in black, wheeling a pram through the air.

At that moment the wind decided to turn nasty. Whistling shrill, it blew down, chill, on the upturned faces in the Market Square, bringing Mrs Pinny whizzing down with it.

Shrieking and shouting, the crowd bundled itself out of the way of the diving pram.

"Move along there! Move along!" cried P.C. Spindleberry, suddenly remembering he was on duty. "Can't you see it's trying to land?"

"What is it, Officer?" said an anxious voice at his elbow.

"Some sort of flying machine," said P.C. Spindleberry. "But whatever it is, it has no business coming down in the Market Square."

"You must arrest the pilot as soon as he lands," said somebody, firmly. "He's probably a spy."

The market place was empty again now. The people had hurried to hide in the alleys or watch from the shelter of the shops.

P.C. Spindleberry took another quick look at the strange black Thing hovering just above his head. There was no doubt about it, it looked exactly like a big, old-fashioned pram. What was stranger still, the Thing that drifted behind it, the Thing that he had thought was a small black parachute, looked exactly like a person.

Dreamily, Mrs Pinny perambulated slowly down towards the puzzled policeman. Then the contrary wind whirled round her again. She was turned, she was lifted, the wind dropped and she drifted into a tree.

Suddenly coming to life, Mrs Pinny put up

one hand and caught at the nearest branch. Then she let go of the pram and hung on with the other hand. The pram fell with a crash and a watery splash into the pool by the fountain. Wheel-deep it fell and right way up. Then, like a boat, it started to float, carrying its cargo of washing through the dark and fishy water, all over lily leaves.

"Help!" cried Mrs Pinny and P.C. Spindleberry stopped thinking he must be dreaming and galloped across the Square.

Under the lime tree where Mrs Pinny hung like a petticoat pegged up to dry, was the statue of General Bunbridge, the founder of the town. He rode with his sword uplifted and his horse for ever half-way over a hurdle.

P.C. Spindleberry hurled himself at the horse and leapt into the saddle in front of the battling General.

"Beg pardon, sir," he said, pulling himself up by the General's beard and holding his sword for support. Boldly now, he put one big boot on the General's outstretched arm and one on his broad stone shoulder. His head was up in the lime tree, not far from poor Mrs Pinny.

"Come on, then, old love," he said kindly, catching her round the waist.

*   *   *

It was over and done, the day was quite gone and night was new in the sky. Someone had rescued the big, black pram and restored it to Mrs Pinny. The spell of the wind was out of it now. It behaved like a proper pram. When it was trundled away with its bundles, it rattled and squeaked as it should. From Market Square to Marrow Lane and by Broadway into Sheep Street went the pram and Mrs Pinny. The Larkins, the Biggins, the Smiths, had their washing returned and Mrs Pinny's purse was plump with pence.

Still half in a daze, she walked through the maze of narrow streets to the station. When the six-fifteen for Tumbleton puffed fussily under the bridge, Mrs Pinny and her pram and Mr Pinny and his bicycle were safely stowed in the guard's van.

In his snug little house behind the High Street, Mr Miskin was sitting down to his savoury tea. "What a lovely day it's been," said his wife. "I got all my washing dry in no time this morning."

"Good thing," said Mr Miskin, taking a meaty mouthful and starting to munch. "It was raining when I came in."

P.C. Samuel Spindleberry came out of the Police Station and stood on the steps for a moment. The blue lamp spilled its chilly, thin light over him, setting his buttons a-sparkle. With a long-legged leap he was down in the street, two and a quarter yards of policeman, counting the height of his helmet, striding towards the fire in his mother's parlour and a plate of buttered crumpets.

In the clutter of cottages at the end of Lambkins Lane, five children had finished their teas. The slanting pencils of the rain were scribbling on the window-pane and the children were cosying close to the glowing coals. Eileen was reading *The Three Bears* to Ronnie while Josie, next door, played Snap with Johnny. Last, but not least, Henrietta, warm, washed and fed, was tucked up in bed, asleep in the thumb-sucking dark.

In Mrs Pinny's kitchen the oil lamp was lighted in the middle of the crimson-covered table and the shadows were all pushed back against the walls.

Mr Pinny was stooping over the stove, making a pot of tea, while his wife sat quietly by in her rocking-chair, her feet, in the floppy felt slippers, resting on the fender. She was still rather shaky, she felt queer and quaky and she wanted nothing to eat.

The curtains were drawn to shut out the night and some of the spite of the rain. It was hurled, like handfuls of grit, at the glass and the windows shook as it struck them. Now the wind was a hound-dog, howling at the door, rattling at the latch and trying to get in.

The old door was jolted, but shut fast and bolted. It would not give way and swing open. After a while the rain-cats stopped spitting and hissing and the wind-hound went whining away.

Mr Pinny spooned sugar into Mrs Pinny's tea and stirred it up for her. Two cups of the blessed brew she drank before she uttered a word. Then

she said, with a sigh, "It's been a queer sort of day."

"Yes," said Mr Pinny and went to the larder to cut himself a slice of boiled ham for his supper.

The Author

Helen Morgan first told her stories to her daughters when they were young because her sight was so bad she could not read to them. Now her gentle, timeless books, many of them illustrated by Shirley Hughes, are read and loved by children everywhere.

The Illustrator

Shirley Hughes worked as an illustrator, and was associated with many distinguished authors, before she began to write her own much-loved picture books. Line illustration is still one of her great enthusiasms. "When you're working on a good text the visual ideas come thick and fast," she says. "With Helen Morgan's rich prose there's a picture in every paragraph. The only problem was in choosing which one to draw."

Shirley Hughes won the Kate Greenaway Medal for *Dogger* in 1977 and in 1984 was presented with the Eleanor Farjeon Award for Services to Children's Books. She is married, lives in London, and has three grown-up children and two grandchildren.